SNAKE HANDLER

FUZZY CAMPER

DEEP-LATRINE DIGGER

CARING BEAR

DONUT DELIVERY

PINBALL WIZARD

NIGHTTIME NAVIGATOR

EVE!
BRIN!

For Judy —BS

For everyone who
remembered to lift the seat
and close the lid when
they were finished —ZO

About This Book

The illustrations for this book were done in acrylic paint on BFK Rives paper. This book was edited by Andrea Spooner and designed by Jamie W. Yee and Saho Fujii. The production was supervised by Erika Schwartz, and the production editor was Jen Graham. The text was set in 718, and the display type is hand-lettered.

WHO WET MY PANTS?

TO EVE + BRIN

WRITTEN BY
BOB SHEA

ILLUSTRATED BY
ZACHARIAH OHORA

LB

LITTLE, BROWN AND COMPANY
NEW YORK BOSTON

I'll get to the bottom of my wet pants if it's the last thing I do!

Look, here's all I know.

This morning I helped out at the lemonade stand.

Then I went for a hike to the waterfall.

Later I fell asleep playing with my tropical fish.

When I woke up, I got donuts and came straight here.

Then...POOF!
My dry pants are wet.
Pants that have never
been out of my sight...
pants I have been wearing
the WHOLE TIME.

YOU MADE YOUR BED, NOW LIE IN IT

LOST SOCK LOCATOR

KNOWLEDGE SEEKER

POISON IVY DETECTOR

FUTURE PODCASTER

EEL FARMER

RENEWABLE ENERGY

FUNGI FORAGER